# LOONIVERSE
## STAGE FRIGHT

### BY DAVID LUBAR

#### ILLUSTRATED BY
#### MATT LOVERIDGE

WITHDRAWN

**BRANCHES**

SCHOLASTIC INC.

ANGIER PUBLIC LIBRARY

# Read all the LOONIVERSE books!

#1 LOONIVERSE stranger things — David Lubar — SCHOLASTIC

#2 LOONIVERSE meltdown madness — David Lubar — SCHOLASTIC

#3 LOONIVERSE dinosaur disaster — David Lubar — SCHOLASTIC

#4 LOONIVERSE stage fright — David Lubar — SCHOLASTIC

# table of contents

For all those marvelous librarians and teachers, including
Sharon Rawlins, Diana Tixier Herald, Teri Lesesne,
C. J. Bott, and many others, who tirelessly spread the
word about my books so I don't have to. –DL

If you purchased this book without a cover, you should be aware that this book is stolen property. It was reported as "unsold and destroyed" to the publisher, and neither the author nor the publisher has received any payment for this "stripped book."

No part of this publication may be reproduced, stored in a retrieval system, or transmitted in any form or by any means, electronic, mechanical, photocopying, recording, or otherwise, without written permission of the publisher. For information regarding permission, write to Scholastic Inc., Attention: Permissions Department, 557 Broadway, New York, NY 10012.

Library of Congress Cataloging-in-Publication Data
Lubar, David.
Stage fright / by David Lubar ; illustrated by Matt Loveridge.
p. cm. — (Looniverse ; #4)
Ed and his friends accidentally sign up for a playwriting contest, a dangerous activity for someone who possesses the Silver Center, and what they write is pretty strange, but when it comes to actually performing the play, Ed's magic coin lends new meaning to the words "stage fright."
ISBN 978-0-545-49608-7 (pbk.) — ISBN 978-0-545-49607-0 (hardback)
1. Coins—Juvenile fiction. 2. Magic—Juvenile fiction. 3. Playwriting—Juvenile fiction.
4. Acting—Juvenile fiction. 5. Friendship—Juvenile fiction. [1. Coins—Fiction. 2. Magic—Fiction.
3. Playwriting—Fiction. 4. Acting—Fiction. 5. Friendship—Fiction.]
I. Loveridge, Matt, ill. II. Title.
PZ7.L96775Ss 2014
813.54--dc233
2013018123

ISBN 978-0-545-49607-0 (hardcover) / ISBN 978-0-545-49608-7 (paperback)

Text copyright © 2014 by David Lubar. Interior illustrations copyright © 2014 by Scholastic Inc.

All rights reserved. Published by Scholastic Inc.
SCHOLASTIC, BRANCHES, and associated logos are trademarks
and/or registered trademarks of Scholastic Inc.

12 11 10 9 8 7 6 5 4 3 2 1                    14 15 16 17 18 19/0

Printed in China                    38
First Scholastic printing, February 2014

Illustrated by Matt Loveridge
Edited by Katie Carella
Book design by Liz Herzog

"Friday!" I yelled as I left school. I was ready for the weekend. I headed down the street to my little brother, Derwin's, school. I always meet him out front so we can walk home together. When I got there, I checked the brand-new watch my uncle had sent me.

I didn't really need to know the exact time, but I liked looking at the shiny silver watch.

One minute and twenty-seven seconds later, Derwin came out and raced up to me, grinning.

"You look happy," I said. "Did you have a good day?"

"It was an awesome day, Ed," he said. "We had an author come read us a story. After that, we saw a movie. It was all about Mars! Then we painted pictures while our teacher read funny poems to us."

Derwin

"That sounds great," I said.

"But then the bell rang, and school was over," he said. "The whole day zoomed away."

I shrugged and said, **"TIME FLIES WHEN YOU'RE HAVING FUN."** I hear people say that all the time. And it's definitely true. Whenever I'm enjoying myself, time zips right past me.

"Time flies?" Derwin asked.

"Absolutely," I said. As I spoke, I felt a tug on my wrist, like someone was trying to lift my arm. The next thing I knew, my watchband had unbuckled itself. The ends started flapping like little leather bat wings.

"No!" I shouted as my watch flew off my wrist and headed toward the clouds. "Come back!"

"Wow!" Derwin said. "I guess time really *does* fly."

The real problem is, I'd found a magic coin a while ago. It's called the Silver Center. And I had to give it to someone known as the Stranger. But it turned out *I* was the Stranger. This coin gave me the power to make strange things happen. I've learned that a little strangeness is good for the world. It helps people come up with new ideas. But, when I'm not careful with what I say, I can end up with too much strangeness — and I can end up without a watch.

Derwin and I walked home. Right when we reached my front door, I heard someone shouting my name. As Derwin slipped inside, I looked back and saw my friend Moose and his older brother, Mouse, heading my way.

"Look!" Mouse said, holding up a flyer. "The town is starting bowling teams."

"The winners get trophies!" Moose said.

"That sounds good," I said. "Let's sign up!"
I liked bowling. I read the flyer. The sign-ups
were at the town hall. That wasn't far.

"Hey, today is the last day to sign up,"
Moose said. "We'd better get going."

"What time is it?" Mouse asked.

I glanced at my watch, then remembered
I didn't have one.

"Where's your new watch?" Mouse asked.

I looked toward the sky. "It's up there, somewhere."

"Time's *up*," Moose said, pointing and laughing.

Then Moose checked his watch. "We only have fifteen minutes. We'll make it, but we better hurry."

# chapter 2

Moose, Mouse, and I hurried into town. We passed the New Curiosity Shop, which sold strange and curious things. The shop owner, Mr. Sage, waved at me like he wanted me to come inside.

"I have to go somewhere!" I shouted. "I'll stop by later!" I hoped he could hear me through the window.

He nodded and moved his lips. It looked like he was saying, "Be sure you do."

I liked talking to Mr. Sage. He'd given me a lot of good advice about how to deal with the Silver Center and all the strangeness it created. But right now, we had a bowling team to sign up for!

As we cut through the town park, we slowed down to watch a bulldozer through the fence.

"That new stage is going to be cool," I said.

"It's called an *amphitheater*," Moose said. "See the sign?"

"Come on," Mouse said. "We can't waste any more time."

I hurried with my friends past the other side of the park, to the town hall.

We got on the end of a long line. "Uh-oh," I said as I thought about the last time we'd stood on line.

"What's wrong?" Mouse asked.

"Do you remember what happened after we waited in line to see the robot dinosaurs?" I asked.

"Sure," Moose said. "One came to life."

"Remember what happened after we waited in line for chocolate bars to sell for our team?" I asked.

"You made me run so fast, they melted," Mouse said.

"And now," I said, "we're in a line again." The live dinosaur and melted chocolate had caused a lot of trouble.

"More fun!" Moose said. "I loved helping with the chocolate."

"More thrills!" Mouse said. "The dinosaur was great."

*More problems?* I wondered. But bowling couldn't cause trouble. Could it?

ANGIER PUBLIC LIBRARY

When we reached the sign-up table, I saw Mrs. Beckett sitting on the other side. She was a coach for one of the town's baseball teams. I really wanted her to pick me for her team this summer. She was both the best coach, and the only one who never yelled.

"Ed, how nice to see you," Mrs. Beckett said. "I'm so glad you're signing up."

"*We're* signing up," I said, pointing to Moose and Mouse. "The three of us want to be a team." I figured she would like that. Coaches love it when kids work together as a team.

"That's wonderful," she said. "I'm sure the three of you will write a fun play."

"Write a play...?" I asked.

Mrs. Beckett nodded happily. My eyes drifted above her, to the signs on the wall.

"Oops!" Moose said. "I guess I need a watch with the date on it."

"I need a watch with anything on it," I said.

"And I need to watch what I eat for lunch," Mouse said, rubbing his stomach as it made a sound like bubbles bursting out of swamp water. "I think I had too many tacos."

"Here's your entry form for the contest," Mrs. Beckett said.

"Uh, yeah. Great." I hadn't planned on writing a play. But I didn't want Mrs. Beckett to think I was a quitter. I put our names and the name of our school on the form, and handed it back to her.

"The winner will get to put on his or her play when the new amphitheater opens, two weeks from today," Mrs. Beckett said. "It will be a very special Friday evening. Isn't that exciting?"

"Sure," I said, trying to sound excited.

"Here's more information about the contest rules," Mrs. Beckett said, handing me another sheet of paper. I stuck it in my pocket.

As we walked out, Moose turned to me and said, "You're on your own."

"What?" I asked.

"This doesn't sound like fun," he said.

"Yeah, it sounds like extra homework," Mouse said.

It looked like I'd be writing the play all by myself. We kept walking until we reached the New Curiosity Shop. "I'll see you guys later," I said. "Hop along without me."

As the words left my mouth, Mouse and Moose each took a giant hop, like super-powered kangaroos.

*At least I hadn't said anything that would make them do something too dangerous*, I thought. I watched Mouse and Moose until they'd bounced out of sight, then I went into Mr. Sage's store.

"Thank goodness you came in," he said. "We have a huge problem."

# chapter 3

# ONCE UPON A MOON

"What's wrong, Mr. Sage?" I asked.

"Have you ever heard of a blue moon, Ed?" he asked.

"I'm not sure," I said. But I had a feeling I'd heard it somewhere.

"A *full* moon happens once every twenty-eight days," Mr. Sage said. "Most months have thirty

THE FULL MOON

or thirty-one days. So, most of the time, there's only one full moon in any month. Understand?"

"Sure," I said.

"If a full moon occurs very early in a month, there's time for a second full moon in the same month," Mr. Sage said. "That second one is called a *blue moon*. Nobody is sure why people call it that, but they do. And people use the phrase **'ONCE IN A BLUE MOON'** for things that don't happen often."

"I get it," I said. "But what does a blue moon have to do with me?"

"Have you noticed that the moon seems connected to strange things that happen to you?" he asked.

"Yes!" I said. "The first time I touched the Silver Center, the moon rose right in the middle of the afternoon. And sometimes, I get the feeling the moon is peeking over my shoulder."

"A very long time ago, people believed the moon could make them do weird things," Mr. Sage said. He tapped his calendar. "We had a full moon two weeks ago, on the first of the month. There's another full moon two weeks from now. I fear that the strangeness you create will get a lot wilder on the night of this blue moon."

"Thanks for the warning. I'll be extra careful that night," I said. It seemed too far away for me to worry about right now. I had a play to write. I turned to leave, then froze. "Did you say *two* weeks from now?" I asked. "*Exactly* two weeks?"

"Yes, the Friday after next," he said. "Is that a problem?"

"Only if I write a winning play," I said. I told him about the contest. "I don't think I'll win. A ton of kids signed up, from all three schools in town. And I've never written a play. But if I win, I'd be on stage in front of a bunch of people when the blue moon rises."

Mr. Sage stared straight at me. "Maybe you shouldn't enter that contest," he said.

"I sort of have to," I said. "But, like I said, I don't think I'll win."

"You might," he said. "The Stranger tends to become very creative since he or she often has to invent clever ways to deal with the strangeness the Silver Center helps make. You'll probably write a very clever play. Be careful, Ed."

"I will," I said as I left the shop. *Time to go home and write a really awful play*, I thought.

# chapter 4

# THE PIRATE HAMBURGER NINJA PLAY

I was surprised to find Moose and Mouse waiting for me in the living room. I could hear Derwin in the kitchen, making a snack. My older sister, Sarah Beth, was playing the piano. It sounded like my little sister, Libby, was dancing up in her room.

"Ready to write a winning play?" Moose asked.

"I thought you didn't want to work on it," I said.

"I changed my mind," Moose said. "I really want to win."

"Why?" I asked.

"I've never won anything," Moose said. "This is my big chance."

"Mine, too," Mouse said. "I want to prove I'm a good actor. But I always get stuck playing small parts in our school plays. Remember last year? I played a tooth. And it wasn't even a sharp one. The best way to get a great part is to write it myself."

"What should we write about?" Moose asked.

"Pirates!" Mouse said. "Everyone loves pirates."

"*We* know they're awesome," Moose said. "But I don't think most grown-ups feel that way. And grown-ups are probably picking the winning play."

Sarah Beth started to play *Twinkle, Twinkle Little Star*. That's when Mouse, who loves outer space, leaped up and said, "Stars! We need to have stars in the play."

"Yeah! Someone could wish upon a star," Moose said. "What should he wish for?"

I swallowed and tried to think fast. I didn't like that this was starting to sound like a good play.

"*Hmmm,*" Mouse said. "He could wish for…"

"A hamburger!" I shouted, tossing out the silliest thing I could think of.

They stared at me. I wasn't going to back down. I started babbling everything that popped into my mind. "No. A kid doesn't wish *for* a hamburger. The *hamburger* makes a wish. That's it! A hamburger wishes that he can run away and join the circus because he's always wanted to swing on the flying trapeze."

Moose opened his mouth. But I talked right over him. "The hamburger gets lost, but he runs into a moose and a mouse who help him."

"I love it," Moose said.

"And the mouse is a pirate," Mouse said.

"Great idea," I said.

"We'd better write this down," Moose said.

I grabbed a piece of paper, and we started working out the first scene. "We'll call it *Bernie the Burger's Big Day at the Circus*," I said.

"Can I help write the play?" Derwin asked, walking in from the kitchen. "I like food, and I like the circus."

"Sure," I said. I figured he'd add some wild ideas.

Sarah Beth joined us after she finished practicing. So did Libby. Then my friend Quentin One came by the house. I have three friends named Quentin — so I call them by number. They always seemed to show up one at a time, and never two or three together. I was beginning to have a hard time telling them apart. They used to look different, but they're starting to look more and more alike. I think it was just another weird effect of the magic coin.

Right after we finished writing the first part, Quentin One dashed off.

A moment later, Quentin Two showed up. He had the idea to add a ninja to the play.

Then, when we finished the second part of the play, Quentin Two left and Quentin Three came by. He wanted to add a giant parrot.

Before we knew it, we'd written a whole play. It was awful.

"We can't possibly lose this contest," Moose said, as he headed home for dinner.

*We can't possibly win*, I thought, smiling.

Normally, I would have been right about that. But not much in my life was normal ever since I'd found the Silver Center and become the Stranger. Even so, if I'd read the information sheet Mrs. Beckett had given me, I might have seen who was judging the contest. Then things would never have gotten as bad as they did.

# LOSING OUT

All day Saturday and Sunday, Moose and Mouse wanted us to polish the play since it didn't have to be turned in until Monday. We actually had fun. I added more really wild things, like a singing toaster, a break-dancing elephant, and a dancing sunflower.

By Sunday night, the play—and the title—had grown longer.

I walked to the town hall after school on Monday to hand it in.

Mrs. Beckett gave me an odd smile and said, "Clever title." After I saw the huge stack of plays on the table, I felt good about our chances of losing. When the blue moon came, I'd be safely in bed, tucked under my blankets.

By Tuesday, I was feeling even better. Lots of kids were talking about the contest. Some of their plays sounded great.

By Wednesday, I was positive we'd lose.

On Thursday afternoon, the whole school got called to the auditorium.

"I wonder what this assembly is about," Moose said as we took our seats.

"Look! There's Mrs. Beckett," I said.

The principal went up on the stage and said, "We have some very special news. As you know, the town held a play-writing contest. I'm thrilled to tell you that the winning play was written by students at our very own Complex Elementary School. Please give a Complex welcome  to Mrs. Beckett, who has some exciting news to share."

*Students*, I thought. The principal didn't say a *student* had won. He'd said *students*. I hoped there'd been another play-writing team. There had to be. There was no way our awful play could have won. No way at all.

Mrs. Beckett came forward and said, "First, I want to thank everyone who entered the contest. And I want to introduce our judges." She pointed to three other people on stage, and told us who they were: "Miss Maribel Martinez from Martinez's Corner Diner, Mr. Roger Chen from Jolly Roger's Used Car Lot, and Mr. Jordan Dalton who works for the World Wildlife Group. Let's give them a hand."

Everyone clapped. My hands moved, but my mind was numb. The judges were a diner owner, a pirate fan, and an animal lover.

"Food, pirates, and animals," I whispered to Moose. "Those judges like all the stuff we wrote about."

"This is great!" he said. "We'll win for sure!"

He waved across the auditorium to Mouse, who was sitting with his class. Mouse gave us a thumbs-up.

"Choosing the winning play was a tough job for the judges," Mrs. Beckett said. "But there was one play they all liked the best, *Bernie the Burger's Big Day at the Circus with Amazing Moose and Mouse the Pirate*."

It looked like my friends and I would be putting on a play to launch the town's new amphitheater. And we'd perform it beneath the blue moon that Mr. Sage had warned me about. Suddenly, I understood exactly what people meant when they talked about "stage fright."

# chapter 6

# FOOD FLIGHT!

At dinner that night, I told my parents about the play. They were thrilled.

"We're so proud of you," Mom said.

"We can help build the sets if you want," Dad said.

"Yes," said Mom. "Since your play takes place at the circus, we could make the circus tent."

"That would be great," I said. "We need stars, a refrigerator, a pirate ship, and a birdcage, too. We'll also need a trapeze for the part about the flying hamburger."

"A flying hamburger?" Mom asked.

"The hamburger wants to be an acrobat in the circus," I said.

"This is going to be interesting," Mom said.

Moose's and Mouse's folks were really excited, too.

"My dad has a friend who owns a big costume shop," Moose told me in school the next morning. "We can get whatever we need—moose antlers, a mouse nose . . . he even has a hamburger suit. It's the perfect size for Derwin. And I'll make sure we get you a really cool outfit."

"That's great," I said. I was going to be the circus ringmaster. And since the ringmaster runs the show, he always has a flashy suit.

As much as I was worried about the blue moon, the idea of wearing a ringmaster costume was sort of exciting.

The amphitheater wasn't ready yet, so we decided to practice at my house after school. But since it was Friday, the 22nd, we went to sign up for a bowling team, before going to my place.

It got pretty crowded in my basement. There were parts for everyone who had helped write the play. It was a fun crowd. My dog, Rex, and my cat, Willow, even joined us.

By the time we finished our first practice, dinner was ready. I guess my dad was trying to be funny, because he made hamburgers.

"I thought this meal would bring the play good luck," Dad said as he plopped a hamburger on my plate. "Though these hamburgers don't fly."

He went to the stove to get more.

Sarah Beth was playing with her burger. I watched as she took some round pickle slices and put them on top of the bun. "Look. It has windows."

"It looks sort of like a flying saucer," I said.

"It needs landing feet," Derwin said. Sarah Beth stuck three carrot sticks under her burger. It started to spin. Then it floated up until it was about a foot above her plate. Everyone stared at it.

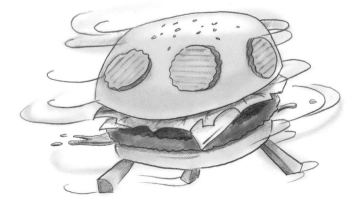

"Wow," Libby said.

I watched it, and wondered what would happen next.

I should have known.

The burger flew across the table, toward the window. Too bad my head was between the burger and the window.

The burger smacked me right in the forehead.

It's a good thing the burger was soft.

Too bad Sarah Beth likes lots of ketchup on her burgers.

The burger bounced off my head and landed on my plate, just in time for my dad to come back and not see anything. Well, he did see one thing.

"Ed, you're a mess. Go change your shirt," he said. "And wash your face."

"One week until the blue moon," I said to myself as I went to the bathroom to wash up. If I wasn't careful, things were about to get much worse.

# chapter 7

# GROWING STRANGER

When I got back to the table, I noticed Derwin was on his second burger. He was having a hard time finishing it.

"Hey, Derwin," I said, "it looks like—" I stopped and clamped my jaw shut.

"What?" he asked.

"Nothing," I said. I was about to tell him something our grandma always said when we put too much food on our plates: **YOUR EYES ARE BIGGER THAN YOUR STOMACH.**

When I thought about my Stranger power bringing that saying to life, I shivered.

I had to be super careful. Look what happened to my watch when I'd said **TIME FLIES**. *I can't use any more sayings*, I told myself. The blue moon was only a week away. I spent a long time thinking about it as I lay in bed that night. I had to be careful to watch what I said, so nothing bad would happen. The best thing I could do was to start practicing right now to think before I spoke.

As I found out the next day, it was hard to keep from saying the wrong thing. I'd never noticed how many sayings could have strange meanings. Here are some of the things I almost said:

1. **I LAUGHED MY HEAD OFF.** I almost said this when I was telling Moose about a funny book I'd read.

**2. CAT GOT YOUR TONGUE?** I almost asked Derwin this when he didn't answer a question right away.

**3. I COULDN'T TAKE MY EYES OFF OF IT.** I almost told Mouse this when we watched an Army helicopter fly overhead.

And that was just on Saturday morning. The hardest part was on Saturday night when Libby asked me for a bedtime story. After I became the Stranger, the things I read to her seemed to come true in messy and even dangerous ways. She looked really sad when I said no. But with the blue moon coming, I couldn't take any chances.

Libby looked even sadder Sunday night. On Monday afternoon, she sulked all the way through our play practice. She was even sadder Monday night, and sulkier Tuesday afternoon. Finally, on Tuesday night, when she looked like she was about to cry, I came up with an idea. "Why don't you tell *me* a story for a change?" I asked her.

"But I don't know how to read," she said.

"You know how to think," I said. "Let's look at some pictures. You can make up a story about them."

"Okay," she said. "That sounds like fun."

I grabbed one of her books, and hoped that this type of storytelling, when *I* didn't do the telling, wouldn't lead to anything strange.

Happily, it worked. Nothing strange happened. I guess Mr. Sage was right. I really was learning to be creative.

Meanwhile, our play practices after school were going great. On Wednesday, my parents made all the backdrops. We took a break from acting to do some painting.

As weird as the script was, and as much as I'd tried to write a crazy play so we could lose, I had to admit performing it was sort of fun. And I was learning to do a better job catching myself before I said anything that could turn strange.

Finally, it was Thursday night. We even wore our costumes for the last practice. It went surprisingly well.

Later, as I sat in bed, looking out at the nearly full moon, I said, "Please don't make trouble tomorrow."

# chapter 8

# BURSTING BALLOONS

Friday evening, we all headed to the park. We reached the amphitheater about a half hour before showtime. Mr. Sage had taken a seat in the last row. While the others went backstage to get ready, I walked over to him.

"It looks like you won that contest after all," he said. "You'll need to be very careful once the blue moon rises tonight."

"That won't be a problem," I said.

"What do you mean?" he asked.

"I've kept my power under control for a whole week," I told him. "I watched every word I said. I didn't make a single strange thing happen. So one more night shouldn't be a problem."

I thought he would be pleased, but his face got as pale as the moon. And his eyes got as big as, well, two moons.

"What's wrong, Mr. Sage?" I asked.

"You didn't stop the strangeness," he said. "You just held it back. It's like filling a balloon with too much air. Sooner or later, the balloon must burst. Be very careful. This could be very, very bad."

"Very, very bad? Uh, maybe we should all go home," I said. "We could cancel the play."

"Ed!" someone called.

I turned around. Mrs. Beckett was standing way down by the front row, with my parents and a bunch of my parents' friends. I guess they'd arrived while I was talking with Mr. Sage. A lot of the other seats had filled up, too.

"Uh, hi . . ." I said, waving at her.

"Time to get backstage!" she called.

Mr. Sage turned toward me and said, "There's no canceling the play with this full house. Good luck."

People were heading toward the new amphitheater from all around the park. It looked like half the town was coming. And, from what Mr. Sage had just told me, all my bottled-up strangeness was in danger of bursting loose at any moment.

I decided to rush through the play as quickly as possible. Maybe we could finish before the moon rose and started causing trouble. As I ran up the steps backstage to join the rest of the cast, I heard the one terrible sound nobody who is about to go on stage ever wants to hear.

# THE SHOW MUST GO UP

I looked down just as I felt a sudden chill tickling my butt. The seat of my pants had gotten caught on a nail head sticking out of the wall.

"Problem?" someone said from behind me.

I knew the voice. It was my mom. "Can you fix it?" I asked. "Quickly?"

She nodded. "I'm sure someone out there has a sewing kit." She dashed off. I stood there, feeling the moon moving closer.

"Got one," Mom said when she came back. She started threading a needle.

"Can't you just pin the rip?" I asked.

She shook her head. "You know the old saying. **A STITCH IN TIME**…"

"**SAVES NINE,**" I said. I'd heard my mom use that saying when she fixed things. I guess it made sense. If you fixed a small tear with one stitch, you wouldn't need to fix a bigger tear later.

But I didn't want to stand there while she sewed my pants. Past her, I saw the very top of the moon peek into the night sky. I wanted to get the play started—and finished—before the moon rose all the way up.

I reached down and grabbed the needle. "I'll finish sewing it," I said.

"Okay," Mom said. "Be careful." She went back to her seat.

I looked at the rip. It was mostly fixed. I didn't have time to figure out how to knot the thread so I stuck the needle through the cloth where it wouldn't jab me. Then I tried to get all the actors together.

The instant I found Moose, he pulled the curtain aside and dragged me out to the front of the stage. The whole audience, who had come to watch the play, could see us.

"Look," Moose said. "Everyone is here. This will be awesome."

I stared at the moon. It was higher—and bluer—with green swirls of mist around it. I'd never seen the moon look like this before! I really had a bad feeling about all of this now.

"We need to get started," I said. I pulled Moose back, and closed the curtain. "Mouse! Libby! Everybody!" I shouted. "Hurry up!"

"We're right here," Mouse said. "Stop screaming."

"I'm not screaming!" I shouted.

"Yes, you are!" Sarah Beth shouted.

"No, I'm not!" This time, my scream turned into a raspy gasp. Between practicing my lines all week and shouting, I'd strained my voice. "Oh, no," I whispered.

"What's wrong?" Sarah Beth asked.

I rubbed my throat. It still felt sore. "I guess I'm a bit hoarse," I said.

Derwin laughed, and said, "Horse! That's funny."

Suddenly, my head felt a lot heavier. "No!" I shouted. Or tried to shout. It came out "Neigh."

I dashed to the makeup mirror. I had a horse's head! True to my words, I'd become a little bit horse.

# chapter 10

# MOONSTRUCK

Just then, I heard Mrs. Beckett, on the other side of the curtain, telling the audience, "Welcome to our new amphitheater. What a lovely evening. And what a lovely moon. It looks like everyone is here. So let's get on with the play!"

The curtain started to open. Moonlight washed over me. Everyone in town was about to see me with a horse's head. I felt myself being pulled toward the moon, which was halfway overhead now. I couldn't even shout for help. I looked at my parents, hoping they could save me.

They sat there as if nothing was wrong. Mr. Sage didn't move, either.

"Everyone's frozen!" Moose shouted.

He was right. The whole audience was as still as a photograph.

"But we're not frozen," Mouse said.

That was true. We could move. But we were also *being moved*! All of us were being dragged across the stage. The moon rose faster. The air around me swirled. My feet had almost left the stage. Just my toes were touching.

I grabbed the edge of the amphitheater, but I couldn't hold on. I flew into the air.

Derwin, Moose, Mouse, and the others swirled around me. I was twirling so fast that the needle came out of my pants leg. It was hanging on by the thread.

There had to be something I could do. But I couldn't talk. Did a *silent* Stranger have any power? Maybe I could use my hands to tell Derwin something.

But what? I had no idea.

Derwin, Mouse, Moose, Libby, Sarah Beth, and the three Quentins were flying around me. We were at least twenty feet off the ground now. I wondered whether we'd get dragged all the way to the moon. There wasn't any air in outer space! Why hadn't we written a play about astronauts? Then, at least, we'd have space helmets.

Derwin pointed at something. I made a grab as it fluttered past my face. It was my watch!

The wind whipped through the tear in my pants, opening it up again. At that moment, everything fell together. There were two sisters, one brother, and five friends swirling in the air. Plus me. It all added up perfectly. I knew the right saying to save all nine of us.

I had to hurry. We were higher, now. The air was getting chilly. Outer space, where we seemed to be headed, was supposed to be very cold. I grabbed the needle and yanked it hard enough to break it free from the thread. I held it up so Derwin could see it. Then I held up my watch.

Finally, I pretended to sew the watch with the needle. The needle was making a *stitch*. The watch stood for *time*.

"Get it?" I asked. I couldn't speak, but I could move my lips. And, with my horse head, I sure had plenty of lips.

"Needle time?" Derwin said. He smiled, as if he'd figured out a puzzle. "Needle little time. You need a little time! Right?"

I shook my head and tried again, making one, big stitching motion.

"Sew far, so good?" Derwin asked. "Umm . . . sew what?"

I neighed out a scream.

"Do something, Ed!" Libby yelled.

"Get us down!" Moose screamed.

"I don't like outer space anymore!" Mouse shouted.

Everyone looked scared, except for the Quentins. I'd never seen all three of them together until now. In the weird, crazy, wild world of the Stranger, that had to mean something. I tried to figure out what to do. It wasn't easy. I was dizzy from the spinning. But, as the three Quentins flashed past me, over and over, I got an idea. It had to work. This might be my last chance.

# MERRY-GO-DOWN

Shivering from the cold, I made the sewing motion again as Quentin One passed me.

I tapped my watch as Quentin Two passed me.

I tucked in one thumb and held out all my other fingers as Quentin Three passed me.

Then I pointed at Derwin. He nodded and shouted, **"A STITCH IN TIME SAVES NINE!"**

I held my breath, wondering whether it would work.

Our spin began to slow. We drifted down like falling feathers.

"It worked," I said as my feet met the stage.

I could hear myself. My voice was back to normal. Luckily, so was my head.

We were standing exactly where we'd been standing when the moon first grabbed us, ready to start the play. I heard a rustling from the audience. They were unfreezing. They had no idea what they had just missed.

"Are you all okay?" I asked the actors.

Everyone nodded. I noticed that Quentin One was there, but not the other Quentins. I wasn't worried. I knew each of them would appear when his turn came.

"Come on," I said to everyone. "The show must go on!"

"Break a—" Moose started to say.

I reached up and clamped a hand on his mouth. I knew that actors said **"BREAK A LEG"** for good luck, but with my powers as the Stranger and this wacky blue moon, I wasn't taking any chances.

We performed our play. I made sure not to turn around. Nobody saw the rip in my pants, and nobody broke a leg.

And, at the end, when we were taking our bows, the audience cheered and broke into applause.

After the clapping stopped, Mrs. Beckett walked up onstage. "Wonderful!" she said, turning toward the audience. "Let's have one more round of applause for our talented young writers and actors." Then, she told us, "Take another bow. You deserve it."

As we bowed again, Mrs. Beckett leaned toward us and added, "You certainly work well as a team. I hope some of you will think about coming out for baseball this summer."

"I will," I said.

"Me, too," Moose said. "Though I want to write more plays, too."

"And act in them," Mouse said.

"Whatever we do," I said, "we're a team."

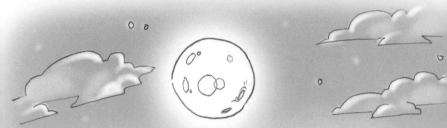

As I ended my bow, I glanced at Mr. Sage, who gave me a thumbs-up and a wink. Then, I looked up at the sky.

The blue moon was still there, but it didn't seem to be a threat to me anymore. I knew I could handle whatever adventures the Silver Center brought into my life. I guess the moon and I were a team, too.

# LOONIVERSE

## How much do you know about Stage Fright?

Look at the **picture** on page 19 and **describe** what is happening.

The root word **amph** means "on both sides" or "around." What do you think the word **amphitheater** means? Reread page 11 and look at the picture for help.

What is Ed's **big plan** to lose the play-writing contest? Does it work?

**Pretend** you have to write a play for a contest. Make sure to include a title, main characters, the setting, and write about two events that take place. Make it as **wacky** as you want!

How does Ed save himself and his friends from the extra **strangeness** caused by the blue moon?

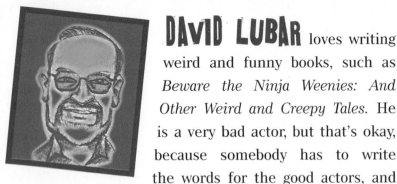

**DAVID LUBAR** loves writing weird and funny books, such as *Beware the Ninja Weenies: And Other Weird and Creepy Tales*. He is a very bad actor, but that's okay, because somebody has to write the words for the good actors, and he'd much rather do that. He once played the bottom half of a giraffe in a play. It was a supporting role. He lives in Nazareth, PA, but he also spends a lot of time in the Looniverse.

**MATT LOVERIDGE** loves watching plays, but the thought of being in one scares him to death. Matt is much more comfortable expressing himself through art than through acting, although he might make an exception if the play was in the Looniverse. Matt lives in Utah with his wife and five kids where all the performances are comedies.